Rapunzel

Key sound short o spellings:
a, o, oh
Secondary sounds: air, ng, ow

Written by Rosie Greening
Illustrated by Clare Fennell

Reading with phonics

How to use this book

The **Reading with phonics** series helps you to have fun with your child and to support their learning of phonics and reading. It is aimed at children who have learned the letter sounds and are building confidence in their reading.

Each title in the series focuses on a different key sound or blend of sounds. The entertaining retelling of the story repeats this sound frequently, and the different spellings for the sound or blend of sounds are highlighted in red type. The first activity at the back of the book provides practice in reading and using words containing this sound or blend of sounds. The key sound for **Rapunzel** is **short o**.

Start by reading the story to your child, asking them to join in with the refrain in bold. Next, encourage them to read the story with you. Give them a hand to decode tricky words.

Now look at the activity pages at the back of the book. These are intended for you and your child to enjoy together. Most are not activities to complete in pencil or pen, but by reading and talking or pointing.

2

The **Key sound** pages focus on one sound, and on the various different groups of letters that produce that sound. Encourage your child to read the different letter groups and complete the activity, so they become more aware of the variety of spellings there are for the same sound.

The **Letters together** pages look at three pairs or groups of letters and at the sounds they make as they work together. Help your child to read the words and trace the route on the word maps.

Rhyme is used a lot in these retellings. Whatever stage your child has reached in their learning of phonics, it is always good practice for them to listen carefully for sounds and find words that rhyme. The pages on **Rhyming words** take six words from the story and ask children to read and find other words that rhyme with them.

The **Key words** pages focus on a number of key words that occur regularly but can nonetheless be challenging. Many of these words are not sounded out following the rules of phonics and the easiest thing is for children to learn them by sight, so that they do not worry about decoding them. These pages encourage children to retell the story, practising key words as they do so.

The **Picture dictionary** page asks children to focus closely on nine words from the story. Encourage children to look carefully at each word, cover it with their hand, write it on a separate piece of paper, and finally, check it!

Do not complete all the activities at once – doing one each time you read will ensure that your child continues to enjoy the stories and the time you are spending together. **Have fun!**

Dot the witch grew magic crops,
like chocolate pods and pumpkin pops.
She planted bulbs and watered seeds
and picked out all the horrid weeds.

Dot the witch likes crops a lot.
She grows some in her flowerpot.

Bob and Dee, who lived next door,
had lots of food, but wanted more.
Said Bob one day, "Let's take a peek
at what the witch has grown this week."

The crops looked tasty as can be.
"Let's gobble them!" cried greedy Dee.
So when Dot popped out to the store,
they grabbed their forks and went next door.

Dot the witch likes crops a lot.
Bob and Dee have got a plot!

7

When Dot came back, she shouted, "NO!
Those chocolate pods took weeks to grow!"
"We're sorry!" Bob cried out in fear.
But then Dot had a good idea.

No! No! No!

She said, "Some help is what I need
to plant my stock of chocolate seeds.
Give me a child, and you'll be free."
"Then it's a deal!" said Bob and Dee.

Dot the witch likes crops a lot.
Bob and Dee are scared of Dot!

Rapunzel was born one hot July,
and very soon, the witch dropped by.
She locked the baby up that day,
inside a tower, far away.

For years, Rapunzel sobbed and cried –
she longed to go and play outside!
"I'll let you go," Dot always said,
"once all these seeds are crops instead."

Dot the witch likes crops a lot.
She locks the girl up on the spot.

There was no time for fun at all –
the heaps of seeds were just too tall!
She'd plant them one by one each day,
until the witch called up to say . . .

"Rapunzel, Rapunzel, way up there:
please let me climb your long, blonde hair!"
The witch would quickly count the seeds,
then drop back down the hair at speed.

Dot the witch likes crops a lot.
She counts the seeds Rapunzel's got.

A few weeks passed, until one day
Prince John saw Dot climb up that way.
"I wonder who's up there?" thought John,
and copied Dot once she had gone.

"Rapunzel, Rapunzel, way up there:
please let me climb your long, blonde hair!"

Dot the witch likes crops a lot.
Prince John decides to copy Dot.

Prince John soon reached the tower's top,
and found Rapunzel with her crops.
They shared a pot of pumpkin tea
and liked each other instantly!

The girl showed John a chocolate seed.
"Once these are planted, I'll be freed!"
"I'll help each day," said kind Prince John,
"until each chocolate seed is gone."

Dot the witch likes crops a lot.
Rapunzel's in a tricky spot.

Rapunzel's job was hard to do,
but it was much more fun with two!
And once the seeds had disappeared,
the duo dropped their trowels and cheered!

But suddenly, the clock struck one.
The witch appeared and spotted John!
"My seeds are gone! You'll pay for this,"
Dot crossly cried out with a hiss.

Dot the witch likes crops a lot.
The clock strikes one and here comes Dot!

Rapunzel said, "Don't worry, Dot.
The prince has helped me plant the lot!"
Dot couldn't help but stop and stare:
her chocolate pods grew everywhere!

"These crops are perfect as can be –
would you two like to work with me?"
Rapunzel smiled and looked at John.
"As long as we're a team, you're on!"

Dot the witch likes crops a lot.
The trio team up in a shot!

Rapunzel and Prince John were wed
beside one of Dot's flowerbeds.

Then, with the witch, they got a shop
to sell their new, amazing crop!

CROP SHOP

Dot the witch likes crops a lot.
The happy pair have tied the knot!

23

Key sound

There are several different groups of letters that make the **short o** sound. Practise them by looking at the words in the flowers and using them to make sentences. Can you use each word in a different sentence?

crop   lot
shop   long   spot
clock   gone

watch   want
what   wand
was

John

Letters together

Look at these pairs of letters and say the sounds they make.

air   **ng**   **ow**

Follow the words that contain air to find a girl with long hair.

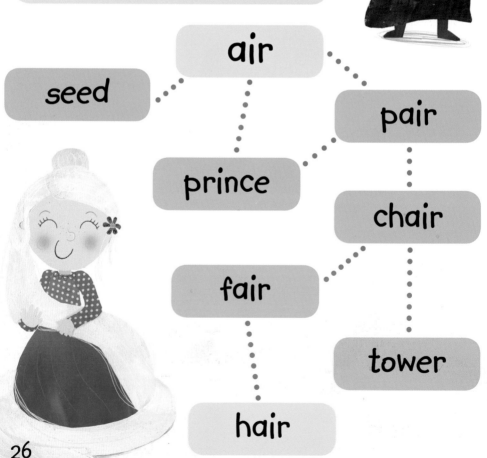

seed

air

pair

prince

chair

fair

tower

hair

Follow the words that contain ng to find angry Dot.

ng

long

plot

amazing

king

work

clock

angry

song

Follow the words containing ow to lead Rapunzel to the tower.

ow

plant

trowel

door

how

flower

lock

tower

Rhyming words

Read and say the words in the flowers and then point to other words that rhyme with them.

drop	hope
crop	
shop	food

stare	share
hair	
climb	child

young	song
long	
count	strong

snow   **grow**   show

witch   baby

girl   **clock**   sock

knock   play

shower   speed

flower

slow   tower

Now choose a word and make up a rhyming chant!

Rapunzel's hair is **long** and **strong!**

Key words

Many common words can be tricky to sound out. Practise them by reading these sentences about the story. Now make more sentences using other key words from around the border.

Dot the witch grew lots **of** crops.

Bob and Dee stole **her** food.

Dot asked for a child **in** return.

not • your • asked • got • he

She locked Rapunzel in a **very** tall tower.

• said • very • a • big • had • made • day • off • we •

Rapunzel had to plant **little** seeds.

Prince John climbed **up** the tower.

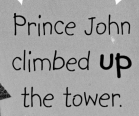

They planted all the seeds together.

The witch **saw** the crops.

Rapunzel got married **to** the prince.

her • saw • in • then • house • the • called • look • my • about • up • you • they •

old • little • like • into • of • with • was • to

Picture dictionary

Look carefully at the pictures and the words.
Now cover the words, one at a time.
Can you remember how to write them?

child

clock

crops

hair

prince

seed

tower

trowel

witch